PUPPY PATROL

TUG OF LOVE

BOOKS IN THE 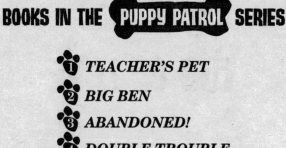 PUPPY PATROL SERIES

COMING SOON

PUPPY PATROL

TUG OF LOVE

JENNY DALE

Illustrations by Mick Reid
Cover illustration by Michael Rowe

AN
APPLE
PAPERBACK

SCHOLASTIC INC.
New York Toronto London Auckland Sydney
Mexico City New Delhi Hong Kong

SPECIAL THANKS TO LORNA READ

No part of this publication may be reproduced in whole or in part, or stored in a retrieval system, or transmitted in any form or by any means, electronic, mechanical, photocopying, recording, or otherwise, without written permission of the publisher. For information regarding permission, write to Macmillan Publishers Ltd., 25 Eccleston Place, London SW1W 9NF and Basingstoke.

ISBN 0-439-11328-8

Copyright © 1997 by Working Partners Limited.
Illustrations copyright © 1997 by Mick Reid.

All rights reserved. Published by Scholastic Inc., 555 Broadway, New York, NY 10012, by arrangement with Macmillan Children's Books, a division of Macmillan Publishers Ltd.

SCHOLASTIC and associated logos are trademarks and/or registered trademarks of Scholastic Inc.

24 23 22 21 20 19 18 17 16 15 14   4 5/0

Printed in the U.S.A.   40
First Scholastic printing, May 2000

CHAPTER ONE

"**S**am is the best dog in the whole world!"

Neil Parker was standing in the middle of a field at the Padsham Dog Show, shouting at the top of his lungs.

His nine-year-old sister, Emily, groaned and ducked down below the table in front of her to avoid being spotted. "Neil, you are *not* my brother. I disown you."

"But he won, Em! Sam came in first in the agility competition and he's *my dog*!" Neil jumped up and down on the spot, punching the air. In his excitement, he didn't care that he had suddenly become the center of attention to the passing crowds. "Aren't you happy for me?" Neil asked, laughing. His short, dark, spiky hair was ruffled, and his T-shirt flapped as he leaped about. "This is Sam's first win. He came in first in his category — by seven clear points!"

"OK, OK, I'm happy for you! But will you stop celebrating! You're eleven not five! And it's too hot to jump up and down. People are *looking* at us."

The day of the Padsham Dog Show was always busy and usually, like today, very hot.

Padsham was a small, country town a few miles from Compton, where the Parkers lived at King Street Kennels. Neil, and his sisters, Emily and Sarah, sometimes felt they were the luckiest people alive. How many other dog-crazy kids got the chance to live at a boarding kennel?

King Street Kennels was situated on the grounds of their house. Bob Parker — Neil, Emily, and Sarah's father — hosted dog obedience lessons twice a week in their converted barn. The Parkers also ran a dog rescue center. They took a booth at the Padsham Dog Show every year to help raise money for it.

Emily dipped her head even lower behind their exhibit table so that only the very top of her brown hair was showing. The wobbly-looking table was piled high with T-shirts, sweatshirts, and doggy stationery. Underneath, Neil's victorious black-and-white Border collie lay in the shade, panting.

Emily glanced at the dog beside her. "Poor Sam. Neil, you've worn him out!"

Sam raised his head from his paws and barked. The dog's feathery tail thumped on the ground. Sam had been the Parkers' family pet for five years. He'd been abandoned as a puppy and was found in very bad condition. Neil had helped nurse him back to health, and now he was a wonderful example of his breed — and a promising contestant at every agility competition in the area.

Neil had been training Sam on an obstacle course at home, and had already entered him in several local dog shows. Sam had been improving with every event and was always highly placed. This was the first time he had actually *won* a competition, however, and Neil was over the moon. Sam had pushed himself over, around, and through the obstacles like an expert.

"Do you have some more water for Sam?" Emily asked her mother, still looking at the tired dog.

Carole Parker was sitting in a green Range Rover parked on the grass behind their stall. All of the doors and windows were open in an attempt to let in some cool air. "After coming in first in the contest, he deserves champagne more than water!" Mrs. Parker remarked. "Here, this is the last of the bottled water."

Emily emptied the water into Sam's tin dish and the collie lapped at it thirstily.

Carole Parker looked at her watch and then began counting sweatshirts. "Two, four, six . . ." They had brought along two dozen, each with the distinctive King Street Kennels logo emblazoned across the

chest, but had only sold one so far. "I might as well put these back in the box. It's getting late."

"I told you not to bother bringing any sweatshirts! It's boiling hot!" Emily flapped her damp white T-shirt to try and cool herself down.

"I sold three notebooks all by myself, didn't I?" five-year-old Sarah said proudly. She was sitting on the grass, drawing a picture of a dog on some scrap paper.

Carole Parker smiled. "Neil, do you think you could get me some more mineral water before we pack up?"

"I want an ice cream!" Sarah piped up.

"Make that two," Emily called out, suddenly standing up again.

"OK," Neil agreed. "I'll go. I know you can't cope with being in the presence of a superstar dog trainer!"

"Neil! Neil!"

Neil turned around and saw Chris, his best friend from Meadowbank School, coming toward him out of the crowd. Chris was wiry and had short dark hair like Neil's. Right now, he seemed to be in a hurry.

"I've just been to the main show ring," he gasped. "You won't *believe* what I've got to tell you."

"Who won the cutest pooch class, you mean? I bet it was one of Mrs. Smithson's Chihuahuas as usual," said Neil, groaning.

"Of course it was! But you'll never guess who came in second!" Chris looked as if he was about to burst and he was trying hard not to laugh.

"Go on, tell me," Neil begged.

Chris dragged the silence out for as long as possible before announcing, *"Sugar and Spice!"*

"Never! I don't believe it!" said Neil, wide-eyed.

Sugar and Spice were two West Highland terriers who had recently stayed at King Street Kennels and caused a lot of trouble. They looked cute and harmless at first glance, but they were actually very badly behaved.

"I think you can take all the credit for that, Neil," his mother said. "This time last year, they wouldn't have sat still on the judging table for five seconds."

"And they'd have bitten the judge!" said Emily.

"Too true. Sam, on the other hand . . ." Neil began.

Emily and Carole Parker groaned.

". . . did even better in the agility contest," Neil continued.

Chris crouched down and played with Sam's silky ears. "Can you escape for five minutes?" he asked Neil, straightening up again. "They've just started judging the Labrador class and it's so funny. Your cousin Steve has entered Ricky — he's causing a riot!"

"This I've *got* to see." Laughing, Neil hurried off with Chris in the direction of the show ring. He called back to his mother: "Won't be long. I'll get the water on my way back."

"And don't forget Sarah's ice cream!" Carole shouted after him. "It'll be torture if you forget!"

Neil and Chris shuffled into a gap between two spectators in the crowd surrounding the small show ring. The dogs were already in the ring, lined up beside a large table. It was quite a big class: Neil counted fourteen different Labradors, all sitting obediently beside their owners. They ranged from puppies to fully mature dogs and were a mixture of different colors — mostly yellow and golden—but two were black.

At the end of the line, Neil's cousin, Steve Tansley, was doing his best to keep Ricky, his pet Labrador, sitting still. It seemed an impossible task. Even though Steve regularly took his wayward dog to Bob Parker's obedience classes, Ricky refused to behave. As Neil and Chris looked on, Ricky kept wanting to stand up and make friends with the dog next to him. Steve had to resort to holding him firmly in place with a hand clamped on the dog's head.

Two judges in long coats were examining a yellow Labrador in the middle of the line. Neil could see that it was a particularly sleek-looking young male. He had bright, eager eyes, an alert look, and seemed to smile at the crowd as his owner lifted him onto the table.

"He looks like a potential winner to me," said Neil, pointing toward the dog as the two judges examined him closely. "Well proportioned. Good grooming. Powerful hindquarters."

"Not too jumpy, either," Chris added, nodding.

"It's all wrong, you know," said a voice, suddenly rising above the chatter of the crowd. "It's cruel putting the dogs through an ordeal like this."

"Eh?" Neil looked around to see who had spoken. The crowd was three or four people deep, and Neil could hear several animated conversations about who should win the competition. "That's not true," he whispered to his friend.

"I wish they hadn't entered him for the show. It's bad for their nerves. It's totally unnatural!"

It was definitely a woman's voice, Neil thought, but he was still unsure of exactly who had spoken among the noisy crowd.

"She seems upset, whoever she is," Chris commented. "I wonder why she bothered coming to a dog show, if that's the way she feels about them."

In the center of the ring, the young Labrador being judged was staring in their direction. Something had caught his attention and his tail was wagging energetically. The two officials moved on to the next entrant, and the dog's owner moved forward to lift him down off the table.

"Nobody could say that dog isn't enjoying himself," Neil observed. "Just look at him! He's reveling in all the attention. That woman's got it totally wrong. Maybe there are one or two high-strung dogs who wouldn't like the atmosphere of a show, but most love all the fuss. They jump at the chance to show off."

The woman from the crowd didn't shout out anything else, and Neil and Chris were soon lost in conversation about the next dog being shown.

After making their own personal list of winners, they clapped and cheered when an impressive-looking black Labrador won, with the happy yellow Labrador awarded second prize.

Remembering that he'd promised to go back and help his mother pack up the booth, Neil pulled Chris away from the show ring and they headed back in the direction of one of the many refreshment tents.

It was four o'clock when they reached the King Street booth again. In the distance, high in the sky above the Padsham showground, billowing black clouds threatened a thunderous end to the red-hot day. Neil was glad his mother had decided to leave an hour before the official end of the show. They had all had enough, and were soon busy packing their merchandise into boxes and loading up the car.

"Help!" Emily cried, staggering under the weight of one end of the collapsible table.

Neil and Chris grabbed the table just before she disappeared beneath it, and they helped Carole Parker maneuver the awkward object into the trunk of the Range Rover. The car had the King Street Kennels logo emblazoned on both of the front doors. Everybody who knew Neil and his family called them the "Puppy Patrol."

Neil picked up another box of unsold sweatshirts. He was maneuvering it around to sit awkwardly on the edge of the trunk, when Chris suddenly yelled, "Look out, Neil!"

A streak of yellow fur shot past Neil's legs and made him drop the box. Instinctively, he thought something was attacking him.

"What was that?" Neil looked in the direction that

the speedy animal had fled. It was a dog, and its legs were moving at such a speed that they were a blur of motion.

"That was close. It almost ran into you, Neil!" said Chris, surprised.

Desperate to find out where the dog was going, Neil and Chris set off across the dusty field and into the parking lot to get a clear view.

"He's running after that car!" Chris yelled, pointing. It was true. The racing dog, which looked like a young yellow Labrador, was pursuing a blue car that was bumping over the grass toward the exit gate. As the car turned left onto the road, the dog continued to run after it. Both boys watched until a tall hedge obscured their view.

"I hope his owners catch him," Emily said anxiously, coming up and standing beside them.

"Right. *I* hope they get him back before he gets in a car accident," said Neil, grimly.

"Poor dog," said Emily.

"Dumb dog!" muttered Chris. "What on earth was he doing, chasing after a car like that?"

"Maybe he's fallen in love with a lady Labrador that was in it," sighed Emily.

"Don't be such a sap," Neil snapped.

Emily made a face behind his back, which made Chris chuckle.

Neil continued to look worried and watched the horizon as distant glimpses of the blue car flashed between the tall trees. "I hope he'll be OK."

CHAPTER TWO

"**C**arole, do we have a gold-plated dog dish?"

Emily dropped her fork and it clattered onto the plate in front of her. "Eh? What are you talking about, Dad?"

"It's for the visitor who's arriving tomorrow." Bob Parker continued eating his evening meal at the big wooden kitchen table, acting as if he hadn't just said something extraordinary at all.

Neil and Carole Parker exchanged curious glances. Sarah giggled.

"OK. Think of a famous dog. One who's won his owners thousands of dollars recently . . ." prompted Bob.

"Muttley! It's got to be!" shrieked Emily.

Sarah clapped her hands and chanted, "Mutt-Mutt-Muttley!"

"Is he really coming *here*?" Neil was suddenly excited at the prospect of such a famous dog staying at their kennels. Muttley had made the local headlines a couple of weeks earlier when he had won a big lottery prize for his owners. They'd been using a system of predicting numbers based on Muttley's erratic barking. The family had claimed their success was all due to him, and the chubby gray mongrel with his floor-mop hairstyle had become an overnight celebrity. He'd been on television and all over the daily newspapers. The media couldn't get enough of him.

"The Hendersons are spending some of their winnings on a cruise," explained Bob Parker. "We're keeping Muttley for three weeks, starting tomorrow."

"I'm not sure we can provide a gold-plated dog dish though, Dad!" Neil smiled.

The past few weeks had been quiet at King Street and Neil was already looking forward to the new arrival. "We didn't make much at the show today," he volunteered. "The sweatshirts were a *bad* idea!"

Bob laughed. "Never mind, I'm sure the Hendersons will pay their way and provide enough to keep Muttley in the manner to which he must have become accustomed!"

Neil pushed his empty plate away. "Speaking of famous dogs. I've got my own superstar who needs feeding and walking. Haven't I, Sam?"

Sam had been curled up on the floor beside Neil's feet and jumped up as soon as he heard his name. He nuzzled Neil with his wet nose, sure that food was on its way.

"Congratulations, Neil. You've done well with Sam. I only hope today is the first of many glorious wins for King Street!" Bob Parker said, smiling.

"So do I!" said Neil, his cheeks reddening slightly. Then he tapped his leg and both he and Sam raced out of the kitchen door into the yard.

Neil's dream-filled sleep was shattered on Sunday morning by the insistent ringing of the doorbell. He'd imagined that he, too, had won the lottery, correctly guessing the six winning numbers by basing his choice on Sam's own unique pattern of barking. The happy thought disappeared in an instant.

Listening carefully, Neil could barely hear his father talking to somebody at the front door. He couldn't stand not knowing what was going on so he jumped out of bed, threw on some jeans and a T-shirt, and rushed downstairs two steps at a time.

His father was talking to a police officer.

"OK, leave him with us. I'll find him a space in the rescue center."

Rubbing the sleep out of his eyes, Neil saw his father take a blue nylon leash from the police officer. He looked down and saw that it was attached to a yellow Labrador. Rubbing his eyes again, Neil studied the dog closely. It looked familiar.

Bob Parker stepped outside with the dog, closing the front door behind him.

Neil snapped to attention, rammed a pair of sneakers on his feet, and followed his father outside.

"Dad! Hang on!" Neil skidded on the gravel path just in front of the rescue center door. "This dog," said Neil breathlessly, pointing to the Labrador. "It's the one from the show yesterday."

"Are you sure?"

"I'm positive. Big happy grin, wagging tail, same yellow coat. I think it won second prize in its section yesterday afternoon."

Bob Parker kneeled down and ruffled the dog's ears. He looked at the Labrador's teeth and ran a hand across its back, then felt its flank and examined all four paws.

"He seems perfectly healthy. A police patrol car spotted him sitting in the middle of the main road between Compton and Padsham last night. It was about ten o'clock, they said. There was no collar."

"Another dog needing a good home?" Kate McGuire, the King Street kennel assistant, arrived on her bike and pulled up alongside them. "Morning, all. Who's this?"

"Morning, Kate. The police have just dropped this

fella off. Neil thinks he's an escapee from the Padsham Show yesterday.

"He was doing a hundred miles an hour down a
road the last time I saw him!" said Neil. "Chasing after a blue car."

Kate looked at the young dog and smiled. "Well,
give me two minutes and I'll help you kennel him.
You can tell me all about it." She wheeled her bike
away to lock it up.

Inside the rescue center, Neil unhooked the mesh
door to one of the pens. There were ten pens in the
center, five on each side of a central stone walkway.
The pens were not that much different from those in
the two kennel blocks next door. Each dog had an
outside run to itself, a basket, and a metal water
dish.

"You'd think he'd have had the sense not to sit in
the road," Neil said, trying to settle the dog down in
his basket.

"He was probably very confused at being lost," Bob
pointed out. "He was hungry and thirsty when they
found him. He doesn't seem too upset by his ordeal,
though, does he?"

The Labrador gave Bob Parker a friendly lick on
the back of his hand.

"There we are." Kate returned and put a dish with
some crunchy dog food beside the dog's basket.

Neil described to her what had happened the previous day.

Kate looked thoughtful. "Do you remember what the dog's name was?"

Neil shook his head. "Sorry. It was one of those long, complicated, pedigree ones and I didn't buy a program. When he ran past us, there were lots of people all shouting different things. If the owner had been calling him, we'd never have heard. You know how busy those shows can get."

"They probably don't print the names of all the entrants, anyway," Bob added. "The Padsham Show's not really that big an event compared to others and there are always lots of last-minute entries. Pity. Otherwise it would have made it a lot easier to find his owner."

"You can call the show's organizers on Monday, Dad."

"Of course. I'm sure we won't have to wait long for the owner to turn up."

"They must be going nuts!" cried Kate. "I'd hate it if my dog ran off like that. Look, he's extremely well-behaved for a young dog. Can't be more than ten months old, I'd say. Anyway, if you'd like to hold him, I'll go and get the camera."

Color Polaroid photographs were taken of every dog that came to the rescue center. The police station in Compton had a regular spot on its public bulletin board for displaying the details of lost dogs. So did the animal hospital owned by the local vet, Mike Turner.

The Parkers were experts at reuniting lost dogs with their owners, or finding good homes for them. If the pictures failed to bring an instant result, Mr. Parker would sometimes give the local paper the details and a copy of the photograph. In the past, the *Compton News* had been great at bringing attention to lost dogs with desperate stories.

"Say 'cheese'!" A bright flash lit up the pen. Kate waited for the dog's photograph to develop, then handed it to Bob, who began blowing on it to help it dry.

"I'll put this in the office. How about some breakfast, Neil?"

"You bet! See you later, Kate." Neil said good-bye to the new arrival, then headed back toward the house with his dad for his favorite Sunday breakfast. He'd already worked up a huge appetite!

After he'd eaten, Neil went with Emily to the rescue center. The Labrador sat up in his basket and whined when they entered his pen. Neil guessed he was overjoyed at seeing people again after his ordeal the night before.

"I'm sure he's the dog from the show. But it all happened so fast. I suppose I could be mistaken."

Emily was looking into the dog's eyes. She rubbed his ears and sighed. "He's wonderful. I hope his owners reclaim him quickly, Neil. He seems happy enough, but I bet he'd prefer to be at home."

"Too true," said Neil. "OK. Time to take Sam for his morning walk, I think."

He walked back across the courtyard. Closing the garden gate behind him, Neil whistled in his special way — one long, continuous sound for about five seconds. At once, the lithe Border collie wriggled out from under his favorite leafy bush and came bounding up to greet him.

Neil ruffled Sam's head, and leaned inside the kitchen doorway to grab his leash. "Race you to the field!"

Neil burst into a run and Sam bolted after him into the clear blue morning.

*   *   *

That evening, just before dinner, Neil was busy
cleaning the pen of an English bulldog who was due
to be picked up the following day. Tank had been a
handful all week and Neil would be very glad to see
him go. As he washed the floor, he decided bulldogs
were one of his least favorite breeds of dog.

He was mentally adding the tenth item to his
"Big list of things not to like about bulldogs"— *they
always made a mess eating their food* — when the
sound of a car on the gravel front driveway caught
his attention.

Neil dropped his mop and went to investigate.

As he came around the side of the house, Emily and
their mother were already engaged in conversation
with a woman who was standing beside her vehicle,
next to a girl and a boy. Neil guessed both were about
nine — Emily's age rather than his own. They looked
excited and the girl was tugging at the woman's arm.

"So, can we help you?" Neil overheard his mother
ask. He wondered what they might want, calling so
late in the evening. It was well past closing time and
Kate had been gone for over an hour.

"Oh, I do hope so," the woman replied. She was
short, and had blond, wavy hair, with bangs flopping
down to her eyebrows. She looked at her bright-eyed
children and then announced, "I think you have our
missing Labrador."

CHAPTER THREE

"**O**h, so he's yours!" Emily burst out.

Sarah suddenly appeared behind her big sister's legs and squealed in delight.

Neil watched as Carole Parker ran a hand through her hair. "You've come about the yellow Labrador?"

"Yes. I'm Pam Weston. We've lost our dog, Jason. A policeman at the station in Compton told me that they'd brought a Labrador to you. I'm sure it'll be him. He belongs to Kirsty and Jonathan here."

Neil noticed that the boy was leaning back against the car. He saw that there was a baby asleep inside, strapped into a baby seat in the back. As Neil got closer, the boy turned to look at him. "You're Neil, aren't you?" he said immediately.

"Yes?" Neil frowned slightly. He knew the face but couldn't place it.

"You don't recognize me, do you?" the boy said accusingly.

"I'm not sure," Neil replied. "Were you at the show yesterday?"

"I'm from school! Jonathan Weston. Kirsty and I are two years behind you!"

"Yeah, right. Is he your dog? The Labrador?"

"We think it's Jason. We've had him for ages. We've got photos of him and everything!"

"I can't wait to get him home again." Mrs. Weston's voice rose above Neil's conversation and distracted him. There was something about it that he recognized.

"Can I pet Jason before you take him away?" Sarah asked anxiously.

"Hang on a moment, Sarah. It's not that simple!" Mrs. Parker was beginning to get a little flustered. "It's quite late and, if it is Jason, there are certain procedures we must go through before we can let you take him, I'm afraid. Are you sure you want to do this tonight?"

"Please, Mrs. Parker. The children missed him so much last night. We were devastated to lose him. And it would be difficult to come back tomorrow."

Carole Parker hesitated. "Well, it might be possible. Can you take the Westons to the rescue center, Neil, while I get some of the paperwork." Carole

Parker took Sarah's hand and together they headed off toward the office.

"This way." Neil led the visitors down the driveway at the side of the house. Emily ran ahead to get the Labrador out of his pen, and they met up in the courtyard.

Emily was holding the yellow Labrador by a leash. He began to bark enthusiastically as soon as the Westons approached.

"Jason! It is you!" Kirsty ran forward and threw her arms around the dog. "I've missed you so much!"

Jason's long, otterlike tail was thumping everybody's legs as they gathered around. The dog smothered Kirsty with enormous licks and then barked excitedly.

"That's our Jason all right!" Mrs. Weston confirmed.

Neil could see that Jason was happy again and he breathed a sigh of relief that the dog had been claimed so soon. Often dogs went unclaimed, and Neil and Emily would have to spend a lot of time looking for suitable new owners.

"How did you lose him, Mrs. Weston?" Neil asked.

"Oh, he just got free from us at the dog show," she replied. "You know how it is. One minute he was there, the next he'd disappeared into the crowd. I was so busy with baby Michael that I just lost track of him."

"How long did you —"

Mrs. Weston interrupted him and pointed at her daughter who was hugging the dog as if she was never going to let him go again. "Kirsty missed him the most, you know."

Emily laughed. "We can see!"

Kirsty held her slender arms around Jason's neck and kissed him on the head. It was a touching reunion.

Jonathan bent down, ruffling the hair on the Labrador's neck, and said, "Welcome back, trouble."

Neil was about to ask his question again when Carole Parker arrived with a clipboard in her hands. Despite the late hour, Neil's mom still looked as professional as ever. Neil would give anything to sound half as confident as she did when *he* was talking.

"We'll need some details before I can release the dog to you. I can't let you take him just like that," Carole said apologetically. "I can see he knows you all, but I need some kind of concrete proof of ownership. Do you have any registration documents?"

Mrs. Weston suddenly looked flustered. "Oh, no, I didn't think we'd need them. Isn't it obvious that Jason belongs with us? You can see how much he loves the children."

"Well, yes, I *can* see that, but maybe you have something else? Photos of you with him, perhaps."

Carole looked over at the dog and felt guilty. Jonathan and Kirsty looked so pleased to be hugging him again and their faces positively shone with happiness.

"Of course, I've got one here." Pam Weston rummaged about in her handbag and produced a crumpled snapshot. "Do you think that's enough, though?"

"Please, Mom . . . can we take him home tonight?" Kirsty begged.

Carole Parker smiled and looked at the picture. Neil glanced at it, too, craning over his mother's shoulder so that he could see it better.

The picture was of Jason and the two oldest Weston children. The Labrador was much younger, perhaps only four months old — but it was undoubtedly him. He had the same sparkling, deep brown eyes and distinctive coloring around his nose. In the middle of the picture, Jason had his paws flopping over the top of a gray stone wall. Neil even recognized the field behind him. It was one of the poppy fields near Badger Farm on the other side of Compton.

"It's a nice picture, Mom," said Neil.

"Yes, it is. I don't think there's any harm in letting you take Jason tonight."

Jonathan and Kirsty Weston cheered. Jason barked a couple of times as if he had understood the good news.

Carole Parker held out her clipboard and a pen. "If you could just write your full name, address, and phone number in the book and sign it, we'll let him go."

"Thank you so much," exclaimed Mrs. Weston as she hurriedly put the photo back in her bag. "We don't live that far away, actually. We're in Sycamore Drive in the new development in Compton. Mrs. Parker, you've made the children so happy again."

"Do you have your own leash for him?" Emily addressed her question to Jonathan but it was his mother who answered.

"Yes, of course, but it's back at the house. I'm sure he'll be OK in the car until then. Anyway, we'd better be going."

She finished writing her address with a flourish of the pen, and then handed the clipboard back to Carole Parker.

Everyone walked back around to the front of the house and Kirsty opened the hatchback of their car. Jason immediately jumped up and settled down onto some big, colorful tartan plaid rugs. Jonathan

slammed the hatchback shut and rushed to the front of the car.

Emily and Neil stood watching them all as Mrs. Weston started up the car. Emily had a wide grin on her face. She had that familiar warm glow inside her that she always got when she was saying good-bye to a dog — especially when it was going home to its proper owners.

Mrs. Weston rolled down the front window and thanked them again for all their help. Carole Parker nodded.

Jonathan waved at Neil from the back of the car.

"See you at school tomorrow!" Neil mouthed at him through the glass.

Jonathan nodded and looked away.

With a screech of tires on gravel, the car pulled out of the drive and followed Compton Road.

Neil turned to his sister, looking puzzled.

"What's up with you?" asked Emily, seeing the look on his face. "Aren't you happy? Jason has found his owners again."

Something was bothering him, nagging away at the back of his brain, but it was nothing that he could identify. He made a mental note to find Jonathan Weston at school the next day and ask him a bit more about Jason. Neil hoped that would shake this weird feeling he suddenly had.

"You alright?" Emily asked again.

"Sorry, yes. It's great news about Jason, isn't it? See you later, I'm going to finish up in Kennel Block One. I was in the middle of cleaning a pen."

"OK."

Neil walked back to the kennels, kicking at the gravel as he went. He was happy about the dog being back where he belonged, but he had the feeling that it was not the last he was going to hear about Jason, the friendly yellow Labrador from the Padsham Show.

"Are you looking forward to seeing moneybags Muttley tonight?" Chris Wilson rattled the loose change in his pocket and laughed. He and Neil were sitting under a tree in Meadowbank School's playing field before classes started on Monday afternoon. "The dog with the amazingly large bank account?"

"You bet I am," said Neil, whistling. "I'm hoping the Hendersons will give Dad a huge tip for looking after their dog so well!"

"Do you think Sam could win the lottery?" joked Chris. "You always said he was one in a million. Now he has the chance to prove it by picking the right numbers for you!"

"I don't think so. Sam's talents lie elsewhere — like in winning agility competitions at dog shows."

Chris groaned. He hoped Neil wouldn't go on about Sam's first competition win again. Chris decided to try and change the subject — fast. "I saw

Emily this morning," he said quickly. "She told me you'd found the people who owned that crazy Labrador."

Neil's face clouded over. "Yes, we did. It belonged to Jonathan and Kirsty Weston — they're two years younger than us. I thought I'd see them this morning but I guess they're not around. I've looked everywhere, though."

"Maybe they're out sick," ventured Chris.

"Both of them? Anyway they were fine yesterday."

"Don't worry about it, Neil." Chris looked up as the bell rang. He stood and brushed himself down. "Come on, we'd better get going."

"I do worry about it, though. I just can't help it."

"You and your dogs, Neil Parker. You can't stop thinking about them for one minute, can you?"

Neil sighed as he followed his friend toward the school building. "No. I can't."

As Neil turned his bike off Compton Road into King Street Kennels, his mother and two sisters passed him in their big green Range Rover and pulled into the front driveway. The drive was already filled up with several other vehicles and Carole had to park the car in a different spot from usual.

Neil was confused. "Hey, what's going on? And what's all the racket for?" The unmistakably loud noise of about twenty dogs all barking at once filled the air.

Emily jumped down from the car and slammed the door behind her. "What do you think? Muttley's here! The other dogs must be going crazy!"

"Mutt-Mutt-Muttley!" Sarah grabbed her bag and ran into the house. Emily rushed after her.

Neil hurriedly leaned his bike against the front wall and followed the noise.

The courtyard between the back of the house and the kennel was full of people. The center of everybody's attention was a proud-looking Mr. and Mrs. Henderson and their scruffy-looking mongrel dog, the lottery-winning Muttley. Mr. Henderson was wearing an expensive-looking suit, and his wife a smart dress, completely inappropriate for visiting a working kennel.

Several newspaper reporters were crowded around asking them questions, each scribbling in a notebook or thrusting a handheld recorder into Mr. and Mrs. Henderson's faces. Neil glimpsed Jake, a photographer from the *Compton News,* who had been very helpful to King Street in the past. He'd often featured stories in the paper about some of the rescue center dogs that desperately needed homes. Above the frantic chatter, the dogs in the two kennel blocks were all barking loudly.

"Wow! There's a TV camera, too!" Emily's jaw dropped.

"I've never seen so many photographers! I hope they don't scare the dogs," said Neil, looking concerned. He realized that Muttley's vacation at King Street Kennels was not going to be as easy as he had thought.

Neil approached the crowd of people and made a "What's happening?" sign at Kate. She was standing beside his father to one side of the group. Neil saw Kate laugh.

Looking between the reporters' bodies, Neil studied Muttley more closely. He was a large, hairy, bumbling animal and Neil suspected he had lots of Old English sheepdog in him. He was terrific, barking on cue and licking the reporters' hands. Muttley also had a way of shaking the hair out of his eyes, which made everybody laugh.

The television camera recorded Muttley being paraded up and down the courtyard and then sitting in his basket in his pen in Kennel Block One.

"This is great publicity, isn't it?" Kate whispered in Neil's ear as they looked on.

"Fantastic!" Neil answered, beaming. "It's the best thing we could have hoped for. They're bound to mention the rescue center as well, aren't they?"

"I only hope we can cope with his expensive habits," Bob Parker chuckled. "He's already caused me one headache this morning."

"What do you mean, Dad?" asked Emily.

"Well, I had to move Dinky, the fat basset hound, into another pen. Mrs. H. insisted that Muttley go into pen eight. Apparently, eight was the first number he predicted on their winning lottery ticket."

"Oh," Emily commented weakly.

"Oh, indeed. You know how much I hate moving dogs in the middle of their stay. It's disruptive. It unsettles them all over again."

"Do you think we need to increase security?" asked

Neil. "Get a few more locks put on in case someone tried to steal him?" He could imagine that Muttley would be very desirable to someone who desperately wanted to win a lot of money.

Bob shook his head. "I'm not sure. Let's see how it goes. Do make sure any visitors have proper appointments, though. We don't want just anybody waltzing in so they can see a famous dog. Once the fuss has died down, I'm sure everything will settle back into the usual routine, and Muttley will be just like any other visitor!"

"I hope so," Kate added. "I can't handle all of these reporters around when I'm trying to work."

Jake overhead her, turned around, and winked.

"No offense," said Kate, turning pink.

"Bob! Bob!"

Neil's mother came rushing up to them. Her face was red and she looked hassled.

"What's up, Carole? What is it?"

"I think you should come to the office right away. We've got another visitor."

"Can't it wait?" Bob Parker turned and looked back at the group of reporters, still busy snapping away and fawning over Muttley and the Hendersons.

"No. We've got a problem," Neil's mom insisted. "There's a man here who claims we have his dog. Or rather, *had* his dog."

Neil exchanged confused looks with Kate.

"What do you mean?" Bob Parker didn't understand either.

"He says Jason, the yellow Labrador, is *his* dog. And that he can prove it. Bob, I think we've given Jason to the wrong people!"

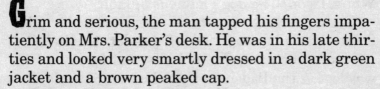

CHAPTER FOUR

Grim and serious, the man tapped his fingers impatiently on Mrs. Parker's desk. He was in his late thirties and looked very smartly dressed in a dark green jacket and a brown peaked cap.

"Sorry to keep you, Mr. . . . ?"

"Scott. My name's Scott," the man snapped back, whipping the cap off his head and scrunching it up in his hands.

Neil shuffled into the office behind his father and mother and tried his best to look inconspicuous.

"My wife tells me that you've come about a Labrador," Bob said calmly.

"Yes, I have. I was informed that you were holding him here. But you appear to have given him away to a complete stranger — without checking out your facts first."

"I'm sure there's been some mistake, Mr. Scott. We always check that a dog is being returned to its rightful owners before it is released. It's King Street policy."

"Is it also policy to get it so wrong, then?"

Neil could see that Mr. Scott was working himself up into a furious temper.

Carole Parker tried to calm him down.

"Mr. Scott, please. Are you sure we are talking about the same dog? I checked its details myself. There was photographic proof of Jason's ownership."

"Photographic proof? Is that all? And Jason? Who's Jason? The dog's name is Junior."

"Perhaps there *has* been a mistake then, Mr. Scott," Neil piped up. "This Labrador definitely answered to the name Jason. I saw that for myself. He was lost at the Padsham Dog Show on Saturday."

"Yes that's right: *I* lost him at the dog show! Look, we're wasting time. I *know* it was Junior. I saw his picture on your wall as soon as I came in!"

Everybody looked at the cork bulletin board on the office wall. In between several small snapshots that were pinned up, Kate's picture of the Labrador was clearly visible. Carole Parker had forgotten to take it down once the dog had left them.

"I've got proof as well, you know. Here's his Kennel Club registration." Mr. Scott produced a bunch of papers from a metal briefcase. "I've got his ownership documents from the SPCA Canine Sanctuary. And some photos of him outside his kennel on my farm. Do you want me to go on?"

Bob Parker took the documents and silently flicked through them. He handed them to his wife for her to review, then flopped back into a swivel chair behind the desk, scratching his beard. "I'm sorry, Mr. Scott. These papers are in perfect order and it does seem that we may have reunited Junior with the wrong people."

Neil couldn't believe it. Nothing like this had ever happened before.

The man looked triumphant. "So what are you going to do about it?"

Bob Parker paused, thinking about what options he now had. "I'll make some inquiries and get back to you as soon as I can."

"Is that *it*?" asked Mr. Scott, incredulously.

"If you'd lost your Labrador, Mr. Scott, why didn't you come to us earlier?" Neil asked him. He didn't like Mr. Scott's aggressive behavior.

"Because I didn't know your rescue center existed! I live some distance away. I had to travel thirty miles to get to the Padsham Show. After Junior ran off, I called the local police stations yesterday, and eventually got your number. It was too late to call or come by last night, so I left it for today. I *thought* he was in safe hands, and didn't think another day would make any difference. Little did I know you'd give him away to the first person who came knocking on your door looking for a new pet!"

"It wasn't like that, Mr. Scott," said Bob, reassuringly.

"How did you lose him, anyway?" Neil asked, pointedly.

"He'd just won second in the Labrador class when something excited him. He just took off! Straight through the crowd. I should have expected it. He's young and still in training."

"Why wasn't he wearing a collar?" asked Carole.

"Bad timing," replied Scott. "I'd just taken off his show collar and was putting his regular one back on when he ran off. I did ask the officials to broadcast an announcement over the PA, but it was a very bad sound system and it was hard to make out what anybody saying. My wife and I spent hours looking for him, but in that crowd it was impossible."

"I see. Yes, the show was very busy," agreed Carole Parker.

"Look, is this really getting us anywhere? All I want is my dog back! I'm sorry I sound so angry, but Junior means a lot to me. Who were the people who took him? Can you tell me their address?"

"I'm afraid not, Mr. Scott," replied Neil's father firmly. "We can't give out personal details like that."

"Then I suppose I'm at your mercy, Mr. Parker. I can't say I'm at all happy about it, but please get in touch as soon as you've made your 'inquiries.'"

Mr. Scott returned the dog's identity papers to his briefcase and clicked it shut.

Neil tried his best to sound hopeful. "I'm sure there's a simple explanation. Labradors do tend to look very similar, and —"

"I should know, I breed them!" Scott retorted sharply, thrusting a business card into Bob Parker's hand. "Here is my information. I'll expect to hear from you soon."

Scott pulled open the door and walked determinedly toward a muddy Land Rover parked on the roadside. He brushed past Kate who was just about to enter the office, and she paused to let him pass.

Neil watched through the office window and saw him drive away.

"Phew — thank heavens we got rid of him!" exclaimed Neil.

Bob looked down at the card and read out loud, *"Paul Scott, registered Labrador breeder, Four Gate Farm, Hadleigh St. Mary."*

"Who on earth was *that*?" asked a confused-looking Kate as she tapped on the door and entered. "He looked mad!"

"He was! Absolutely fuming! We've lost his dog, Kate!"

Neil was wide-eyed and looked at his parents to see how they were taking it all.

"I can't blame him for being angry. It must be a very frustrating situation for him." Bob Parker swiveled in his chair to face his wife and put his head on his hands. It was the first time Neil had seen his father look really worried about kennel business.

"I can't help feeling a little guilty," confessed Carole. "I should have known not to let the dog go with just a single photo as proof. I should have asked for his purchase documents. But it was late, I'd had a long day, and the Weston children looked so thrilled to see him. I can't understand it. Jason, or whatever his real name is, looked so comfortable with them — as if he'd known them all his life. It doesn't make sense!"

Kate looked at Mr. Parker. "This isn't going to look good for King Street's reputation, is it, Bob?"

"No. Not at all," Mr. Parker agreed thoughtfully. "All the more reason to straighten it out quickly. We need to find out some more background about this dog. I think I'd better give Mrs. Weston a call right away. I don't want to spoil her children's fun, but the sooner we find out what's going on, the better.

"And Kate. Can you get rid of those reporters? The last thing we need right now is for this thing to leak to the press!"

"So he was really mad then?" asked Chris as he admired Muttley through the wire mesh of the dog's pen.

"Mad wasn't the word for it. At one point I thought I saw veins popping out of his forehead!"

"I'm glad I missed him. I tried calling right after school to see if I could come by, but the line was busy. It took me ages to get through."

"It's all these reporters," sighed Neil. "They all want to see Muttley. It's been a madhouse around here ever since I got in."

Muttley responded to the sound of his own name with a series of loud barks.

"Hey! We should have written those down, Neil. Maybe they would have won us a prize," chuckled Chris.

"Don't *you* start!" Neil retorted with a grin. "Emily's been scribbling away ever since he got here. Anyway, I'm beginning to think the lottery is a waste of money. Dad never wins anything!"

"But it worked with the Hendersons," Chris reminded his best friend.

"Just a lucky coincidence, that's all," Neil snorted. "Dad thinks he's going to win us enough to build an extension on the kennels, but I can't see it ever happening. Our luck has just run out, anyway."

"Because you've lost the Labrador, you mean?"

"What a mess. Remind me to ask Dad if he had any luck getting in touch with Mrs. Weston."

"Remind me about what?" Bob Parker appeared over Neil's shoulder.

"Oh, Dad. I was wondering how Mrs. Weston reacted when you told her about Mr. Scott. What was her explanation?"

"I'm afraid I'm still getting no answer. I couldn't get hold of her earlier on, and she doesn't have an answering machine. I've tried three times already."

"They might have just stepped out," said Neil, hopefully.

"For this long? On a school night? No, I suppose I'll have to drive over there and drop a note under their door."

Neil and Chris immediately looked at each other. Maybe they could help?

"I'll see you later, boys," said Mr. Parker as he left the rescue center.

"Chris?" asked Neil, slowly.

"Yes, Neil?" replied Chris, innocently.

"Why don't we go for a bike ride?"

"Not out over the other side of Compton, by any chance? To a certain address where a fugitive dog is holed up avoiding capture?"

"*Right*. We can check out the Westons' house and see if they really *are* in. They might be deliberately not answering the phone. Come on."

"Hang on, Neil, I can't come!" Chris sighed. "I promised Mom I wouldn't be too long. I've still got homework to do."

"Oh. I'll get Emily to come with me. Shame, though. You're going to miss all the fun and excitement!"

"Don't I know it!" Chris said good-bye to Muttley and followed Neil outside. He waved to his friend and rode off down Compton Road toward home.

Neil looked around for his sister and spotted her in the backyard with Sam.

"You're coming with me!" Neil said as he pulled his sister away, out of view of the kitchen windows.

"Hey!" protested Emily. "Where are you taking me?"

"You'll see!" Neil said mysteriously, thrusting Emily's bike into her hands. "Come on!"

Dodging past the office window on their bikes, the

two riders biked down Compton Road, pedaling as fast as they could.

The Westons' home was in one of the newly developed parts of Compton, where rows of modern houses had been built.

Neil and Emily rode around looking for the right street. All around they could see small front gardens with bushes and flowers that were struggling for survival in the heat of the day. After five minutes, they turned left at the end of Hazel Street and found themselves on Sycamore Drive.

"Do we know what number it is?" Emily asked, leaning over her handlebars and surveying the long road in front of her.

"Sorry, Em. Couldn't give the game away by asking Dad for the address, could I? He'd never have let us come here on our own. Let's pick a house and ask."

Neil approached the nearest front door and knocked. Seconds later it was answered by an elderly woman with curlers in her white hair. "Yes? Can I help?"

"Excuse me, we were wondering if you knew where the Westons live?" explained Neil.

The woman looked blank.

"They have three children. Two kids about our age and a baby," he added.

The old woman still looked blank. Neil was beginning to think she was a bit deaf.

"And they have a dog. A yellow Labrador," Emily added. She looked at Neil hopefully.

"Ah, of course! Jason. He's been playing in the road with them two kids all day."

Neil and Emily both breathed huge sighs of relief.

"But you'll have to be quick, you know," the woman continued.

"What do you mean?" asked Emily.

"Why, they're moving today — if they haven't left already. Look, that's them going now!"

Neil followed the woman's bony finger in the direction she was pointing. At the other end of the street, a large white van was just pulling away from a small bungalow.

"Oh, no! Hurry, Emily!"

Quickly thanking the old woman, they set off up the street.

But it was no use. Even before they'd reached halfway, the van was picking up speed and turning the corner out of sight. They'd never be able to catch it.

They stopped outside the bungalow, panting from their efforts — which all seemed to have been in vain.

"I don't believe it!" groaned Emily.

"No wonder Dad couldn't get hold of them. They were in the middle of moving!"

Emily stooped down and picked something up off the ground. "Neil, look, it's a dog's rubber bone. From what that old woman said about seeing Jason, and with finding this bone . . ."

". . . it all confirms that he was here, Emily. And you know what? I think they've stolen him!"

CHAPTER FIVE

Bob Parker was not in the best of moods when Neil and Emily arrived back at the kennel. The first thing Neil heard was his father complaining about Muttley.

"Having that dog here is an absolute nightmare!" he grumbled, pacing up and down the kitchen. "The phone hasn't stopped ringing today. The whole world seems to want to come and see him!"

"Calm down, Bob," said Carole Parker, soothingly. "Eat your dinner. It'll be quieter tomorrow."

Emily looked at Neil and smiled. "*You're* telling Dad about the Westons moving away, Neil, not me!" She grabbed both bikes and wheeled them away toward the garage. "I'll put the bikes away!"

Neil rolled his eyes. "Thanks a lot."

He breathed deeply and went inside the house to give his dad the bad news.

Carole Parker looked up from eating her dinner. "The wanderers return. Where have you two been all this time?"

"Sycamore Drive," he replied sheepishly.

"Sycamore Drive? Isn't that where the Westons live?" Carole asked, giving Neil a concerned look.

"It *was.*"

"Explain yourself, Neil," said his father, sternly. "Why did you go out there? I thought you'd taken one of the dogs out."

Neil sat down at the table and began to eat his food, fresh from the oven.

"You were so busy with Muttley, we thought we'd see where they lived. See if anyone was around. But when we got there, we'd just missed them."

"They were out again? I was going to go over there this evening," said Bob incredulously.

"No, they were moving. As in *moving away!*" It was Emily who answered as she came in and sat down at the table.

Bob Parker's expression clouded over. "Are you sure? You actually saw them leave?"

"In a big moving van! We looked in the windows of their bungalow and it was completely empty. It looked like they left in a hurry, too," confirmed Neil.

"Great. This is all I need. I'd better call Mr. Scott immediately and let him know it's going to take a lit-

tle bit longer than we thought to get his dog back."
Bob pushed back his chair and left the room.

Moments later the rest of the family could hear
the sound of Bob Parker's soothing tones on the telephone in the hallway.

"How did he take it, Dad?" Neil asked tentatively
when he returned.

"He wasn't exactly pleased, but then I didn't *exactly* tell him what we'd found out about the Westons, either. He's definitely holding King Street
responsible though, which is my biggest worry."

Emily shook her head. "I still think Jason belongs
to the Westons. He looked so at home with them,
didn't he, Neil?"

Her brother frowned. "I'm not so sure, Em. Mr.
Scott seemed to know what he was talking about. He
was the one who was showing Jason on Saturday, after all. Mrs. Weston didn't even mention the Labrador class. Chris and I didn't pay much attention to
Jason's owner when we were watching — but it was
definitely a man. And the Westons' behavior is a bit
suspicious, isn't it? Moving the day after they dog-
nap Jason."

"Absolutely," said Bob, sighing. "Anyway, Mr. Scott
wants me to go out and see him at his farm. I said I'd
go tomorrow."

That night, Neil lay on his bed, exhausted, with Sam
curled up beside him. He kept thinking about what

might happen to the missing Labrador. As he stroked the Border collie's ears, Neil tried to picture how affectionate Jason had been with the Weston children. He tried to conjure up the picture they had showed his mother to prove that he was theirs. He heard Mrs. Weston's voice again, thanking his mother for letting them take the dog home the previous night. Her voice sounded familiar . . .

Neil rolled over and drifted off to sleep. The last picture in his mind was the image of Mr. Scott's angry face. Mr. Scott wanted his dog back very badly indeed. But now the Labrador had disappeared. How on earth was King Street Kennels going to get out of this mess?

* * *

"The Westons? They're no longer with us, Neil. They've moved and they've been withdrawn from school."

It was Tuesday morning and Neil couldn't believe his ears. The school secretary's words were confirming his worst fears. "So they're not coming back? Ever?"

"No. They've moved out of our district," she replied, turning away.

"Oh. Thank you, Ms. Thorn." Neil trudged back outside into the morning sun. He found Chris sitting underneath their favorite tree in the school playing field.

"Any luck?" Chris asked hopefully.

"They've gone, all right. Thorny said it was a bit sudden, but they've definitely gone. Jonathan and Kirsty have been withdrawn from classes. Their teachers have all been told about it!"

"So you're stuck then," concluded Chris.

Neil scratched his head and looked thoughtful.

"Looks like it."

"Do you think your dad will go to the police?"

"As a last resort," Neil replied. "I think he wants to see this Scott guy first at his farm. He's driving out there tonight, after we close, and I'm going to see if I can go with him."

Chris nodded. "He might not be the sort of person you'd want to give the dog back to, anyway. Pretend you've found the dog, but that you don't think Scott is a suitable owner. If he breeds them, and takes them to shows as well, he might be in it just for the money. You know — a bit cruel."

Neil wasn't so sure. "No, I think he's fairly professional. He seemed to know what he was talking about when he came to see us. Anyway, we'll see tonight. I'll call you when we get back."

"Good luck!"

CHAPTER SIX

The Parkers' Range Rover pulled off the main road and turned onto a side lane that led to Mr. Scott's farm. A large wooden sign at the entrance was painted with the words: FOUR GATE LABRADORS — BREEDING, SALES, AND PURCHASE. PROPRIETOR: PAUL F. SCOTT.

At the end of a short driveway stood a large Victorian farmhouse. It had rough white walls and tiny windows. Mr. Scott appeared in the doorway before the car had come to a stop.

Neil noticed that he looked more casual and relaxed than when he had visited King Street. He was wearing brown corduroy trousers, green Wellington boots, and a checked shirt. He took off his cap and welcomed them. Out of sight, Neil could hear the loud cacophony of several dogs barking together.

"Glad you could make it," said Mr. Scott. "Come through the house. I'll show you around the place while we talk."

"Thank you." Bob Parker turned to Neil and Emily and smiled, indicating that they should follow him in.

Mr. Scott introduced them all to his wife, who was in the kitchen. She was a plump, pleasant-looking woman with curly brown hair and an infectious smile. She immediately insisted on making refreshments for the three visitors and promised that they wouldn't take more than a few moments to prepare.

"I'm sorry my husband shouted at you on the phone," she said to Bob Parker. "He doesn't often lose his temper. The dogs are his life, you know. He's very protective of them."

Paul Scott coughed. "This way." He led them outside to where the dogs were housed.

As Neil approached two low, brown buildings, he could sense that the farm was a very professional establishment and very well run. There were fences everywhere, and neat stone walls — there was not a rock out of place. The fields surrounding them on all four sides were luscious and green, thick with trimmed grass.

"These are the kennels. I don't think you'll find my dogs lacking basic comforts and the freedom to run around." Mr. Scott opened the main door and led them down a sandy walkway between two long rows of pens.

All the dogs were out of their baskets and barking at the visitors. Some of them pressed their wet, black noses up against the wire mesh and whined.

Neil noticed Labradors of several different colors — almost as many shades as he had observed at the Padsham Show. They were kept in well-lit, clean, and spacious pens with generous outdoor runs — twice the size of the ones at King Street. They had comfortable baskets, too, and all looked healthy and very well cared for.

Emily poked her fingers through the mesh door of one of the pens and cooed. Inside was a litter of puppies, all chocolate-colored — one of the rarest shades of the Labrador breed.

Emily was entranced. "Aren't they gorgeous!"

"These little ones are only one week old," said Mr. Scott, affectionately. Neil sensed that he was very proud of them.

The mother lay sleepily in her basket. She lifted her head and her bright, brown eyes shone. The three little puppies tumbled over one another and bounced playfully off their mother.

Neil's father was visibly impressed. "The whole place looks very efficient, Mr. Scott. I've been working with dogs for twenty years now, and I've rarely seen anywhere as well run as Four Gate Farm."

"Thank you, Mr. Parker. I'm sure King Street usually runs very smoothly, too. Let's go back inside and discuss our small . . . problem."

Bob Parker's face reddened a little as they followed Mr. Scott back into the house.

Mrs. Scott announced that the refreshments were ready and led them over to a big wooden kitchen table covered in a summery cloth.

"How long have you been in business, Mr. Scott?" asked Neil, diving into a slice of chocolate cake. Mr. Scott wasn't at all how Neil had expected him to be.

Mr. Scott thought for a moment. "My parents have always kept Labradors. My mother started breeding them, so I could say I've been in the business all my life. I managed to get this place started up based on her reputation. We have a good track record for breeding pedigree dogs. I also train them for showing. I get a lot of fun out of it, and it helps the business."

"Are dogs just a business for you, or do you keep any as pets?" Neil wanted to know.

Mr. Scott let out a throaty chuckle. "Drop any crumbs under the table and you'll soon get your answer to that question!"

Emily pulled up the tablecloth and peeped underneath. "Neil, look! It's a fat dog!" She couldn't resist pulling off a small chunk of cake and holding it under the table.

The graying muzzle of an elderly black Labrador came into view, and he greedily ate the cake from Emily's hand.

"We don't normally let our animals become house dogs — but Barney here's a bit of an exception, isn't he, Paul?" Mrs. Scott remarked to her husband.

"He was our most successful stud dog. He sired several champions. When we retired him, we just couldn't let him go. He's the only one I've ever kept. He has such a lovely personality, so we invited him indoors to share our lives. He's a bit on the heavy side now, as you can see. Cake is his biggest downfall, as Emily has already found out! But we all love him to pieces . . . don't we, Barney?"

Mr. Scott played with the dog's ears and stroked him under the chin.

"The other dogs all stay outside. They're well

trained, are kept on good diets, and get lots of exercise. We spend a fair amount of time just giving them love and attention, too. It's my secret ingredient, if you like. I have three paid members on staff here most days. Happy dogs breed happy puppies, don't you think?"

He addressed the remark to Mr. Parker, who nodded in agreement.

"I couldn't agree more. We have one house dog, like you," answered Bob. "But we never bring our rescued dogs indoors. We don't want them to get attached to us when they're destined to be adopted by other people. It's not fair to the dogs."

Neil started to relax, and he decided to tackle the thorny subject of the missing dog before his father did. "When did you get Junior, Mr. Scott?"

"Ah, Junior. He's one of my favorites. If it had been any other dog but him, I don't think I'd have made half as much fuss. We didn't breed him. In fact, we got him from the SPCA. My cousin's son happens to work at one of their canine sanctuaries and he let me know that they'd gotten a pedigree Labrador pup in. He knew I'd be interested.

"We're always on the lookout for new blood for our breeding stock and, rather than always going to the same places, we thought we'd try something entirely different."

"A random factor," said Neil, understanding what Mr. Scott was getting at.

"That's it, exactly. Sometimes it works and you get champions out of it. Sometimes it doesn't — and you get pups that can only be sold as pets."

Bob Parker nodded.

Mr. Scott continued. "Junior was about four months old when we got him. It was earlier this year. I could tell he was going to be a large dog, and he was completely untrained. But he had good conformation, super looks, and a lovely character — so I decided to take him on. After a bit of training he fit in quite well, though he was never very happy in a pen. He preferred to be running around free."

Neil was thinking that the description sounded exactly like Jason.

Mr. Scott continued the story of Junior's background. "He was too young to start his career as a stud dog. As you know, they need to be fully mature and that won't be till he's two or so. Junior is a dog who is easily bored. As he loves people so much, and enjoys showing off, Maggie persuaded me to start showing him in the meantime. The Padsham Dog Show was his first big public appearance. . . . The rest you know."

Mr. Parker coughed. "Indeed. Yes, we do."

"I can see why you were so upset to lose him." Neil was touched by the man's devotion to his newest dog.

"And you haven't had any luck contacting the people who've taken him?" Paul Scott looked Bob Parker in the eye.

"Not yet. I'm having difficulty getting through to them."

"I'm not surprised. I bet they were professionals. They probably spotted Junior at the show and deliberately lured him away. If I ever find them, I'll definitely prosecute."

"I don't think it is like that, Paul," said Bob, quietly. "It was actually a young family who claimed the dog. The children obviously knew him."

"Whatever. Whoever it was, I think we've both been taken for a ride, Bob."

Their discussion was interrupted by the shrill ring of Bob Parker's cell phone.

"Excuse me, Paul. I'll just have to get this." He got up and stepped outside.

As Neil and Emily continued chatting to Mr. Scott about Junior, they could hear their father's voice outside, talking into the phone. It was getting louder with every sentence.

Everyone turned to look at Bob Parker when he came back into the kitchen. His face was pale.

"Neil, Emily, get in the car. We've got to get back to King Street. Immediately!" His voice was stern and serious.

"Dad, what's up? What's wrong?" Neil was immediately very worried.

"Anything I can help with, Bob?" Mr. Scott added, obviously concerned.

"No, it's too late. The police are already there."

"Police? Dad, what's happened?" Emily was frantic with worry.

"There's been an incident at the kennels. Some kids tried to take Muttley. Kate has been hurt."

CHAPTER SEVEN

As the green Range Rover approached King Street Kennels, Neil felt the blood drain from his face. Blue flashing lights lit up the sky above the Parker house and sent a thrill of anticipation down his spine. Emily gripped his hand tightly in the backseat.

Everybody was in the kitchen. Kate was sitting at the table, clutching a mug of hot tea. She was in tears. Most of her blond hair had escaped from its normally neat ponytail and tumbled down over one shoulder. There was an unsightly red mark on her forehead where somebody had hit her, and the beginnings of a large bruise on her left wrist. She wiped her eyes with the back of her other hand. Carole Parker had a comforting arm around Kate's shaking body.

Two uniformed police officers stood behind them. One was scribbling in a notebook.

"Are you alright, Kate?" Bob Parker rushed toward Kate and sat in the seat next to her.

Carole Parker tried to fill them in as quickly as she could. "They forced the side gate, Bob. Luckily, Kate was able to set off the alarm, and they ran away."

"I think it confused them," Kate added with a sniffle.

"Sam was a big help, too. He never stopped barking at them." Carole stroked the frightened woman's shoulder.

"It was terrifying," Kate gasped. "I've never been so scared. There were about five of them. Sam was awesome. He knew there was danger right away and wouldn't give them a moment's peace. They rushed at me while I was in Kennel Block One. I tried to keep the door shut but they all shoved past me. One of them hit me." Kate lifted a hand to her sore forehead.

"We've taken a statement, Mr. Parker."

Neil recognized Sergeant Moorhead and smiled weakly, then he bent down and gave his Border collie a scratch on the head to say "Well done."

"Did you catch any of them?" Emily asked anxiously.

Sergeant Moorhead shook his head. "I'm afraid they all escaped. Sam gave one of them a few teeth marks on his arm, though. It sounds like they were drunk and didn't care who they hurt. They definitely weren't local — Kate heard their voices. Probably came down from Manchester after hearing about Muttley."

Neil was shocked. "Trying to steal him, you mean?"

"And they just had to pick the exact time when none of us were here," Bob Parker said grimly. "The main thing is that Kate is safe."

"We might still get them," said the other officer, trying to sound confident. "There's a patrol car combing the area now. With a little luck they won't get far."

"I hope not," said Bob.

"Those locks in the kennels will be needing some attention, though. They made a total mess of a couple of them."

Carole Parker agreed. "There's at least two that will need replacing completely. We wouldn't want anybody trying to steal Muttley again!"

Emily was horrified at the prospect that somebody might try to grab their prize canine visitor again.

"Muttley! This is all his fault!" Bob Parker slammed his fist down onto the kitchen table and startled everyone.

"Dad?" Neil said quietly. "What do you mean?"

"He'll have to go. I'm not putting Kate or anybody in this family at risk again."

"But where will he go?" asked Neil.

"To Uncle Jack's. He and your aunt can keep him in their house until his owners get back."

Neil was confused. "You mean hide him?"

"Exactly. The Hendersons will understand. We're just not geared up to taking phone calls from journalists every minute of the day, and to having people traipsing through the place all the time. King Street is a working boarding kennel, and having Muttley is too much. It's upsetting everything. Can you understand, Neil?"

Neil stayed silent.

"I agree with your father, Neil," said Carole, soothingly. "Look at Kate. Look what she's been through! We don't want this happening again, do we?"

"I understand. It's tough on Muttley — but I understand." Neil fought to control his mixed emotions. He was upset that Kate had been frightened, but sorry to see that Muttley had to suffer because of it. The dog would be unhappy locked up in a house all day. He wouldn't be able to go out for long walks in case somebody spotted him and told the newspapers where he was.

"I'll call the twenty-four-hour locksmith," said Carole.

"And I'll give Jack a call. I'm sure he'll help out." Bob turned to Kate. "And if you're OK, we'll have Sergeant Moorhead give you a lift home."

The police sergeant nodded. "No problem. We're

done here. I'll get one of the boys to give you a call if we catch those thugs."

As the kitchen slowly emptied of people, Neil was left sitting at the table with Emily. Tired from all the evening's excitement, Sam lay curled up in his basket. His legs began to twitch.

"Look, he's dreaming!" said Emily, smiling.

Neil grinned weakly. "Good old Sam. He must be worn out. I wonder how Junior's getting on — wherever he is."

"Neil, you've started calling him Junior!" exclaimed Emily.

"Oh, I suppose I have. I think it's because I was so impressed by Mr. Scott's place tonight, Em. I really believe he loves that dog."

"So do the Westons, Neil. We both saw that," Emily replied.

"It's confusing, isn't it? All I do know for sure is that we've got to move fast on this," Neil said thoughtfully. "Otherwise Mr. Scott will feel letdown. He'll think we're just not bothering. We've got to find that Labrador before the Westons take him too far away. It'll help Dad, too — he's so busy with this Muttley thing already."

"But what can we do?" Emily asked. "Try the local paper?"

"Not a good idea. I think we'd best keep reporters out of Dad's sight right now, don't you?"

Emily managed a laugh.

Neil looked thoughtful. "Dad's going to be wrapped up with getting the locks fixed, repairing the damage those thugs did, *and* getting Muttley away tomorrow, isn't he? So it's up to us to find out where the Westons have gone. Agreed?"

Emily nodded.

"Meet me tomorrow right after school. Tell Mom that you have to go to practice or something."

"OK, but why? Where are we going?"

Neil suddenly looked very sly. "We're going back to Sycamore Drive."

The Westons' old bungalow on Sycamore Drive wasn't as empty as Neil and Emily had thought it would be. As they rounded the corner at the end of the road, there was another big moving van outside the house.

"Neil! They've come back!" cried Emily, astonished. It was the last thing she had expected to see.

Neil didn't reply at first and studied the van closely. He wasn't so sure. "False alarm, Em. It's a different van! It looks like somebody else is moving *in*."

"Oh. But that's good, isn't it?" Emily replied. "They might have a forwarding address for Mrs. Weston."

Neil knocked on the door of the bungalow and a young man answered. He was wearing paint-spattered jeans and had a dusty cloth in his hand.

"Sorry to bother you," Neil began. "But the people who lived here before, the Westons, do you have a forwarding address for them? It's quite, er, important that we get hold of them."

The man shook his head. "Sorry. They didn't leave anything — except a mess."

Emily was disappointed and her face clouded over.

"You could always try the agency that rents the house out," continued the man, trying to be helpful. "They might know. But I doubt it. The place was a real mess when we got here. They seem to have left in a hurry." The man rummaged around in his pockets and brought out a card with a telephone number on it. "Here. Try this number. Good luck — you'll need it!"

Neil took the card and thanked him. The door

closed behind them as they stood looking down at the number on the card.

"It's a chance, Neil."

"A *slim* chance. Come on. Let's get back home before they miss us. I'll sneak a call from the upstairs phone while everybody is having dinner."

"Neil! What have you been doing upstairs all this time? Your dinner is nearly cold!"

Neil slipped into his seat at the kitchen table and avoided looking at his mother. He looked up momentarily and winked at Emily. He wanted to let her know that he'd successfully made the call to the agency.

Bob Parker was talking about Muttley.

"What about Muttley?" asked Neil. "Where is he? Has he gone?"

Across the table, Sarah giggled. "Cloth ears!"

Carole Parker looked exasperated. "If you'd been here on time, Neil, you'd know that Uncle Jack came over today and took Muttley away with him."

"It certainly cheered Kate up, Neil!" Emily laughed.

"Why? Was it funny or something?" asked Neil.

"Hysterical! Apparently, Dad had to cover him with a blanket and smuggle him into the back of Uncle Jack's van." Emily laughed again, imagining how silly it had looked.

Bob Parker couldn't help but smile.

"Dad? Is this true?" Neil was having trouble believing that they had gone to such lengths in order to move Muttley.

Bob's smile grew larger. "There was somebody hanging around outside. Near the gates. I thought he was a reporter, spying!"

"It was probably some perfectly innocent man walking into Compton and stopping for a breather!"

Everybody burst out laughing.

Carole Parker cleared the plates from the table. "It did look very strange, I must admit."

Neil took the opportunity to signal to Emily that she should follow him upstairs. They left the kitchen without anybody asking them about their after-school activities and rushed upstairs to Emily's bedroom.

Neil flopped down onto the bed below a huge poster of some TV animal-show host that Emily had pinned to the wall.

"Well?" asked Emily, breathlessly. "What did the agency say?"

Neil's face didn't give anything away. "There's good news and bad news. Which do you want first?"

"Stop messing around! Give me the bad news."

"OK. The agency doesn't have an address for the Westons, either. I think the woman I spoke to was hoping *I* would tell *her* where they were. She got very excited when I told her why I was calling."

"What did she say?"

"Only that Mrs. Weston *did* leave in a hurry. She left owing rent and the place was a mess. There were dog hairs everywhere! I think she was a bit miffed because there was a 'no pets' rule."

"Then we're still no nearer to finding the new address, Neil. So what's the good news?"

Neil hesitated and raised his eyebrows. "The good news is that I've thought of another surefire way of getting it."

"I'm waiting," said Emily, tapping her foot.

"We can get it from school. Thorny is bound to have it, isn't she? Mrs. Weston can't just pull her kids out of school without telling them where she's off to."

"Neil, you're brilliant!" Emily clapped her hands in pretend admiration.

"True. But the bad news is —"

"Hey! We've already had the bad news!" Emily cried.

"I know, but there's more. I lied. Old meany Ms. Thorn will never give it to us, will she?"

"She might."

"She won't," said Neil, forcefully. "Not in a million years. I'll try, of course. But you can imagine what she'll say." Neil began to mimic the school secretary's voice. "I couldn't possibly give you that information, Neil Parker. It's confidential. It's more than my job's worth. Blah blah blah."

Emily started laughing.

Neil suddenly looked serious. "So . . . we'll probably have to break in to the school and get it!"

CHAPTER EIGHT

Neil tapped nervously on the school secretary's door and waited. The longer it took for Ms. Thorn to answer the door, the worse the mood Neil suspected she would be in.

"One, two, three . . ." He tried counting to make the time pass by faster.

"Anything I can do, Neil?"

Neil's blood froze at the sound of the principal's cutting voice. He turned and looked up.

"I was looking for Ms. Thorn, sir. I needed . . . an address."

"She's not in this morning, I'm afraid. Or in tomorrow. She'll be back on Monday. I'd help you myself, but that filing system of hers is a monster. It's completely Jurassic. I'd get lost in there if I tried. No, it'll have to wait until next week. Sorry!" The principal was off down the hallway before Neil had had a chance to reply.

Emily shuffled out from her hiding place in the janitor's closet and rushed over to him. "What did *he* want?"

"It doesn't matter," said Neil hurriedly. "What matters is that he told me Ms. Thorn is going to be off for the rest of the week. Paul Scott didn't give Dad that long to find out about his dog. So . . ."

Emily hesitated. "So . . . we go to plan B."

"We do. We break in and get it ourselves. It's the only way."

"When?"

"Saturday morning. There's a soccer game going on. The school will be open but there'll hardly be anybody around."

"What if we're caught, Neil? Dad will flip."

"I know. I'm terrified, Em. But this is the only way I can think of getting this address. We'll take Sam with us. If anybody stops us, we can say we were looking for our dog!"

"It *sounds* like it might work. You're right, Neil. We've got no choice. If we don't find the Westons, Mr. Scott will find *us*, and King Street will be in even bigger trouble!"

*   *   *

The next evening, Neil and Emily dropped their bikes on their cousin's lawn and shouted through the mail slot in the front door of the house.

"Anybody home? It's the Puppy Patrol!" they chorused.

The door opened and out onto the porch came a bedraggled-looking Steve Tansley. He was thirteen — two years older than Neil — and went to a different school.

Steve pushed his dark floppy hair out of his eyes and grunted. They both assumed he had said hello.

Behind Steve's legs, his wayward Labrador, Ricky, panted energetically, his big pink tongue lolling out of the side of his mouth.

"Are you OK?" Neil asked, looking concerned.

Steve looked at him and sighed. "Sure. Just tired, that's all."

"Ricky worn you out again?" inquired Emily. "I'm not surprised. My dad tries so hard with that dog. I think you've got to face it, Steve. Ricky is beyond hope!"

"No, no, it's not Ricky. It's Muttley! Come and see, he's in the garden." Steve pulled the door shut behind him. He led Neil and Emily around the side of the house and into the large garden beyond.

Neil was suddenly struck by an alarming thought. "Hang on a minute. If Muttley's in the garden, won't people be able to see him? They might recognize him!"

"Not anymore, they won't."

"What do you mean?" asked Emily.

"See for yourself." Steve pointed toward a gray, hairy animal with two magenta-colored bows tied on its head, kicking up turf on the lawn. His coat was trimmed and beautifully groomed and the hair on his head was neatly parted.

Emily stared at the dog and frowned. "Muttley?"

"Er, Muttella, actually." Steve looked sheepishly at Neil.

"Steve! What have you done to Muttley? You've turned him into a girl!" Neil's jaw dropped.

"It was the only way we could get him out of the house without people recognizing him, Neil. He went crazy inside — breaking everything that wasn't nailed down. You didn't tell us that he was so clumsy!"

"Sorry, Steve. I didn't know. He was fine in the kennel while *we* had him."

"Anyway, he may be out of the house, but now he's digging up the garden all the time. I've been running around like a madman trying to get him to stop, but he just keeps doing it somewhere else. I can't win!"

Muttley looked up from his digging and barked. The bows on his head flopped down in front of his eyes, and the dog had to shake his head to flick them away again.

"How's Aunt Mary taking it?" Emily asked tentatively.

"Not very well. I think she's going to call your dad tonight and ask if he'll take Muttley back."

"Oh, no!" cried Neil. "She can't! I can help you with his digging problem. If you shake a really noisy tin in his ear every time he digs, he'll soon begin to associate the sound with digging — and he should stop. I've seen Dad do it with other dogs."

"It's no use, Neil. Mom's made up her mind. The dog's got to be out of here this weekend at the latest."

Neil looked at Emily and shrugged. "Your turn to tell Dad!"

Neil and Emily skirted the edge of Meadowbank School's playing fields, trying desperately not to look too conspicuous. Every now and again, Neil threw a short stick for Sam to chase after and retrieve. The black-and-white Border collie scampered back and forth collecting it and dropping it obediently at Neil's feet.

In the middle of the school playing field, a soccer game was in progress. Emily and Neil pretended to watch, and cheered every time somebody scored a goal.

"Are we going in the front way or the back way, Neil?" Emily whispered, attaching Sam's leash to his collar.

"I thought the side door near the hall. It'll be unlocked and there shouldn't be anybody hanging out around there," replied Neil.

They reached the school building without incident. Before they went in and set off down the long corridor that led to the school secretary's office, they both took a careful last look around. The school was silent, and there was a faint smell of polish in the air, mixed with cleaning fluid.

"Quiet now, Sam. Shh!" Neil held his finger to his lips and the dog knew that this signal meant he wasn't to bark.

Treading softly — with their hearts racing and nerves tingling — and alert to the slightest sound of anybody who might be approaching, Neil and Emily began what felt like an endless journey down an ever-lengthening corridor.

Finally, the door of Ms. Thorn's office was in front of them, and they came to stop. Neil felt a jolt of nervous excitement run through him.

"On guard, Sam!" Neil whispered.

The lithe black-and-white dog sat down outside the door, his ears cocked and alert. Neil turned the handle and the door swung open.

"How did you know it was going to be unlocked?" Emily asked incredulously.

"It's never locked. Too many of the teachers need to go in and out of here all the time. It's the filing cabinets we have to worry about. Quick! Inside!"

He and Emily ducked into the room and closed the door behind them.

"We'd better not knock anything over, Em," Neil whispered. "As long as we stay quiet and don't let anyone see us through the window, we should be alright. Sam'll bark if he sees anybody coming."

"Where do we start, then?" whispered Emily.

Neil looked around and took in the layout of the room. He'd been in here a few times before, on errands, but he'd never stopped for more than a minute. Nobody stopped longer in Ms. Thorn's office than they absolutely had to.

Behind a large flat black desk with a cluttered top was a whole wall of gray filing cabinets. Various sets of stacking trays full of paper and textbooks were on top of the cabinets.

"You start at that end, and I'll do this end. Read out loud what it says on all the labels," Neil instructed.

"OK." Emily skirted around the desk but then noticed a framed photograph propped up in one corner. "Hey! Old Thorny's got a dog! Look, Neil, it's a Doberman pinscher!"

Neil quickly looked at the picture his sister was holding up of Ms. Thorn with her arms around a powerful black-and-tan guard dog. "Somehow I'm not surprised at her choice of breed. Dobermans can be quite vicious as well, sometimes."

Emily laughed and carefully put the picture back on the desktop — exactly as she found it. She started to read out the file names. "Suppliers, A–Z, Book Clubs, Personnel Agencies, Requisition Forms, Staff Records —"

"I bet that one's locked!" interrupted Neil. "Go on, try it."

Emily tugged on the top drawer and it rattled noisily.

"Told you. Nothing here," said Neil, scanning the cabinets in front of him. "What's next on your end?"

"Lost Property, Pupil Records! Yes!" Emily let slip a little cry.

"Excellent!" Neil moved over to join her in front of two five-drawer filing cabinets standing side by side, each labeled PUPIL RECORDS.

"How do we get into these things, anyway?" asked Emily, giving each of the drawers a fruitless tug. "We don't have the keys."

"Aha! No problem. Ms. Thorn keeps the keys in one of her desk drawers," Neil said, grinning triumphantly.

Emily was astounded. "How on earth do you know that?"

"Hasheem told me."

"You told Hasheem we were breaking into Ms. Thorn's office? The whole school will know about it on Monday! One of the teachers is bound to find out, and we'll be expelled. Neil, how could you?" Emily put her face in her hands and moaned.

"Keep your hat on, Em! Hasheem told me ages ago. He'd been in her office last term and saw her get them from her desk. Look, I'll show you." Neil stood behind the desk and bent down. "They're in one of those thin, funny drawers." He felt underneath the lip of the desk. "They don't have handles. Ah, here it is. You just push it," he said, giving a rectangular section of one panel a shove. "And out it comes. *Voilà!*"

Emily looked up. "Great! But hurry up, Neil — I'm getting worried."

Neil quickly picked up a ring with six or seven thin, silver keys on it and rapidly tried each of them in the first lock. Eventually, one was a perfect fit, and the top drawer slid effortlessly out on its rollers, revealing a dense collection of files and folders.

"The W to Z files are in here," Neil said, sliding open the bottom drawer. "Wallis, Warwick . . . Weston, J! Yes, this will do!" He pulled out a bulging manila file.

"It's Jonathan Weston's confidential file. Ms. Thorn would go crazy if she knew we were doing this." Emily peered out of the window. She glanced back nervously at the closed office door. "I hope Sam hasn't fallen asleep."

"Look, it's here! Jonathan's old address has been crossed out and a new one written above it. It's in Colshaw, on the other side of Padsham. They must be going to Colshaw All Saints School."

"They haven't moved *that* far, then. Is there a telephone number?"

Neil flicked on a few pages. "No, but did you know how he did on last year's geography test? He only —"

"Neil! We haven't got time!" Emily was getting more nervous the longer they stayed in the office.

Neil wrote the address down, swiftly replaced the file in its correct place, and closed the filing cabinet drawer. He locked it and replaced all the keys in Ms. Thorn's desk.

Suddenly they heard a bark outside the door.

"Someone's coming!" Neil tucked the piece of paper with the Weston's new address on it into his back pocket and rushed toward the door.

Emily had just managed to close it behind them before an authoritative voice snapped, "Neil Parker? Emily? What are you two doing in here with a dog?"

It was the principal.

Emily's face turned white and Neil had trouble keeping himself from shaking.

"Nothing, sir," Neil mumbled. "Our dog got into the school and we were trying to get him back."

Emily looked down at Sam, and slid her foot over next to his flank. She nudged him gently, and the dog stood up and scampered off toward the door they'd used to enter the building.

"He's off again, sir! Sorry about this! We'll just go and get him!" Emily glared at Neil and set off after the collie.

"Er, yes. We've got to go and get him back, sir," Neil

mumbled again. He started running after Emily and Sam, who was streaking away down the corridor.

"Make sure he doesn't get into the kitchen, Neil!"

Neil could hear the principal shouting something at him, but he didn't care. They got ahold of Sam, crashed through the double doors at the end of the corridor, and tumbled onto the edge of the playing field, laughing.

"Phew! That was close!" Emily cried.

"Good dog, Sam!" Neil ruffled the Border collie's fur and praised him, then clipped his leash onto his collar.

"Sam was great, Neil. He did everything perfectly."

"He's an absolute star."

Emily was still panting from having run so fast. "Mr. Scott will be so impressed when we tell him we've found his dog, won't he?"

"He sure will," Neil agreed. "This time tomorrow we might even have Junior back where he belongs. Wherever that is!"

CHAPTER NINE

Colshaw was a fifteen-minute bike ride from the Compton town center. Neil and Emily set out from King Street on Saturday afternoon, calculating that the whole journey would take them no more than about half an hour.

Emily looked over at her brother as they free-wheeled down a hill on Compton Road. "Do you think we should have told somebody where we were going?"

"This is something we've got to fix ourselves, Em," Neil shouted back into the wind. "You saw how Dad reacted when Uncle Jack called and told him he was bringing Muttley back. He looked so stressed."

"He did look kind of preoccupied, didn't he?" Emily

couldn't help but agree with him. "Did you bring the street map?"

Neil tapped one of the bulging pockets of his jacket.

They rode on in silence for the rest of the journey, only stopping twice: once to get their breaths back after a particularly steep climb, and the other when they were so lost in the maze of streets in the middle of town that they had to consult their map.

"We're almost there. It won't take long." Neil folded up the map and put it back into his pocket.

Emily bit her lip. "What are we going to say to them when we get there?"

"We'll tell them what Mr. Scott told us," Neil said matter-of-factly. "He got Junior from the SPCA and has certificates to prove it. Then we'll tell them that they've got to bring him back to King Street."

"What if we've come all this way and they're not in?" Emily asked.

"There's a fifty-fifty chance that they are," Neil began. Suddenly his eyes lit up. "But it doesn't matter either way. Look over there!"

Walking down a tree-lined street, Neil had spotted a woman with a stroller. Alongside her was a familiar-looking girl, a boy, and a yellow Labrador dog.

"It's the Westons! And Junior!" gasped Emily.

"Jonathan!" Neil shouted across the road. "Over here!"

Jonathan Weston stopped in his tracks and his mouth gaped open like a fish. He tugged at the sleeve of his mother's baggy blue shirt. She shot Neil a horrified look, and then immediately looked down at the Labrador. Junior, meanwhile, was tugging on his leash and pulling in Neil's direction. The dog had spotted a familiar face and wanted to say hello.

Neil and Emily pushed their bikes across the road and walked slowly up to the Westons. There was a stony silence for what seemed an eternity to Emily before somebody spoke.

Mrs. Weston's blush rose up to meet her blond bangs. "Neil Parker, isn't it?" She looked down at the Labrador again and half smiled. "Have you come about Jason?"

"Yes. I'm not sure that what you told us about Jason is true, Mrs. Weston," said Neil, quietly.

There was a silence as the woman stared at him. Then she ran her hand through her blond hair and sighed.

"OK. You win. Come back with us, Neil. I'll explain everything."

Pushing their bikes, Neil and Emily accompanied the Westons back to their new house in the adjacent street. Jonathan described it as a "proper house"; they had more bedrooms, a bigger kitchen, and a large back garden as well as a small front one.

Neil and Emily settled themselves on the comfy

sofa in the Westons' living room. Emily kept looking at Neil and wondering how they were going to say what they knew they had to say. Two large patio doors opened out on to a sunny, unkempt garden. It was ideal for the dog to run around in.

"Sorry the place is such a mess," said Mrs. Weston as she entered the room. We haven't been here a week yet, and there's still so much to do." She placed two mugs of tea and a plate of cookies down on a low table and said, "Help yourselves."

"Thanks." Neil leaned forward and picked up a mug.

Jonathan and Kirsty Weston sat cross-legged on the floor. Both had their hands on the Labrador, who sat calmly between them. The dog seemed sad and was strangely quiet. He stared straight ahead at Neil and Emily, which unsettled them a little.

"Does Jason really belong to you, Mrs. Weston?" asked Emily, looking away from Jason.

Neil stared at his sister. She'd just said exactly what was on his mind.

Mrs. Weston bit her lower lip. Her eyes left Emily's and darted awkwardly around the room. "Yes — and no," she replied at last.

"You obviously weren't total strangers to him," said Neil. "He knew you all. Otherwise he wouldn't have been so happy to go off with you the day you came to claim him."

"It's very complicated, Neil," Mrs. Weston said,

sighing. "You see, Jason *used* to belong to us. When he was a puppy."

Neil nodded. It made sense that there was already a special bond between them. No dog could pretend to know people when he didn't.

"We got Jason because Jonathan and Kirsty wanted a puppy," continued Mrs. Weston. She sat back in her armchair. "I didn't know at the time that I was pregnant with Michael. When he was born, Jason wouldn't leave him alone. He was always licking the baby's face and trying to play games with him. I think he thought Michael was another puppy. Jason was such a lively pup — far *too* lively for that tiny house we were in. He was always knocking things over and breaking them."

Neil thought of Muttley and his aunt. Some dogs just weren't made for cramped houses with lots of fragile things. Or babies!

Mrs. Weston continued her story. "One day, I went into the baby's bedroom. I'd left the door open so that I'd hear him if he cried. Jason had gotten in. When I arrived, he looked as though he was trying to climb into the crib."

"You must have been very frightened," said Emily, sympathetically.

"I was. I know he was only trying to play with Michael, but I was worried in case he accidentally hurt him. I panicked, rushed down to the SPCA, and explained that we just couldn't keep Jason. Naturally, the kids were very upset."

Jonathan and Kirsty both nodded.

"So what happened then?" Neil asked.

"Well, a few weeks after Jason had left, I spoke to a friend about it and she told me that there are things you can get to put over cribs to prevent animals from getting near a baby. She also said that he could be trained to be better behaved, and not lick faces and throw himself at people."

"That's true. I could have done that for you," agreed Neil.

"I might have come to you if I'd known King Street was so close! Anyway, seeing how upset the children were, and knowing that there were things I could do to protect Michael from Jason, I decided that we should get him back again. I suppose I missed him, too. He's the most lovable animal I've ever known."

"And the most loving!" Kirsty said, beaming.

"Yes, he is. However much affection you give that dog, he gives even more back. He's one big love factory, aren't you, Jason? You know we're talking about you, don't you?"

The yellow Labrador padded over to Mrs. Weston and rested his head against her knee. His eyes closed in bliss as she played with his silky ears and scratched his head.

"See what I mean?" said Mrs. Weston, in a voice husky with emotion.

How are we ever going to take him away from them? thought Neil. It would be heart-wrenching for them all.

Emily was touched by their story, too. "Why couldn't you get him back?"

"Weeks had passed by then. When I went back, he wasn't there. I was so upset I decided we should get another Labrador puppy quickly, to help us forget Jason. That was how I found Mr. Scott."

Neil was astonished. "You know Mr. Scott?"

"Yes. I'd heard about Mr. Scott being a breeder, so we went up there — and found Jason, penned up in a cage. He wasn't for sale, though. Oh, he looked so miserable. He went wild when he saw us. I didn't dare reveal that we were his previous owners, in case Mr. Scott thought I was irresponsible. The kids had trouble not letting on we knew him."

"I almost called him Jason at one point. Right in front of Mr. Scott!" said Jonathan, laughing.

"Anyway, having seen Jason again," said Mrs. Weston, "we couldn't bear to have any other dog. I must admit, Mr. Scott's dogs were all pretty expensive, too. I didn't expect them to cost that much."

"We didn't know what to do, did we, Mom?" said Kirsty, excitedly.

"Then we went to Padsham Dog Show," said Mrs. Weston, "and saw Jason there. It was the last straw. Jonathan and Kirsty really had to drag me there, too. I usually hate dog shows. I think they're such an ordeal for the dogs."

Neil's mind was racing. He remembered watching the Labrador class being judged, and a woman shouting out from the crowd. It must have been Mrs. Weston!

"It was wonderful that he came in second, of course," she continued. "Though I couldn't bear to look at him being examined like that —"

"And we just wanted to take him home with us," Kirsty interrupted.

"At the end of the show, I gave him my special whistle, and I know he recognized it. He looked straight at us!" Jonathan said. "But then Mom said we had to go. I looked back and Mr. Scott was doing something to Jason's collar. He was still looking at us. I was sure of it."

"Then we went to the parking lot," concluded Mrs. Weston.

"So Jason must have gotten loose and run after you," said Neil.

Emily guessed the next bit. "But he got there a little too late because you were already driving off."

"If only we'd known!" Mrs. Weston sighed. "We could have simply opened the car door and he'd have jumped in. I was so desperate to get Jason back at that point, I really would have done it. We could have avoided getting King Street Kennels involved."

Neil was serious for a moment. "You know that would have been wrong?"

"You really would have been accused of stealing him, then," Emily told her.

Mrs. Weston gave a guilty grimace. "It wouldn't have been very honest, no. But I was thinking about Jonathan and Kirsty. And I wanted what was best for Jason. I was confused."

Neil looked puzzled. "But how did you find out that King Street had him in the first place? You didn't know he'd run off from Mr. Scott when you drove away."

Mrs. Weston nodded. "No, it was an absolute stroke of luck. The following day I was talking to my neighbor, who'd also been at the show. She'd seen a Labrador run off into the crowd and knock a show judge over in his excitement. She thought it was the funniest thing she'd seen all day. That's the only reason she mentioned it. I called the police station right away and, sure enough, a Labrador had been found and taken to King Street."

"We knew it was Jason," said Jonathan, enthusiastically. "He's so clever! He was looking for us!"

"If you'd loved a dog as much as we love Jason, Neil, wouldn't you have been tempted to do the same thing?" Mrs. Weston looked pleadingly at Neil and Emily.

Neil took a sip of his tea. "I suppose I might," he admitted. "But claiming Jason as yours *was* wrong. Dad's in trouble with Mr. Scott, and I know he's going to want answers."

"Mr. Scott is coming to the kennel tomorrow morning, Mrs. Weston," said Emily. "When he finds out we know where the dog is, he'll want him back, I'm afraid."

"No! He can't! Jason's ours!" Kirsty Weston cried, and flung herself at her mother, sobbing. Jonathan grabbed hold of Jason and held him defiantly.

"We really have to work this out," Neil said quietly.

"I think you should bring Jason around to King Street tomorrow at eleven-thirty."

The Westons looked glum. They sat quietly and let the news sink in. Kirsty moved over to Jason and patted him affectionately on the head.

By that time the following day, Jason's fate would be decided. And Kirsty Weston might have to say some painful good-byes to her dog all over again.

CHAPTER TEN

"**W**here did you find the Westons' new address, Neil?"

Carole Parker sat at her desk in the kennel's office on Sunday morning. It was judgment day and Jason's fate would be decided before noon.

Neil turned away from his mother, looking guilty. "From school."

"We should have thought of that. But you know how it's been this last week, Neil. Having Muttley has been a nightmare. I thought we'd solved the problem, but now he's back again! And the calls from reporters have started all over again."

Neil was relieved that his mother had accepted his vague answer to her question, and was more than happy to move on to a new topic of conversation! "I think I'll go and see him now," he said hurriedly. "I know he was trouble and caused Dad a lot of headaches — but I'm glad he's back."

"Don't tell your father that!" laughed Carole. "Anyway, well done, Neil. You and Emily have been fantastic. I'll see you later when Mr. Scott arrives."

Neil left his mother to her work and walked over to Kennel Block One. On his way, he stopped by the barn and looked in on the obedience class, which was in full swing. He stood just inside the entrance and

spotted Emily watching her dad putting an American cocker spaniel through its paces.

"Ugly things, aren't they?" whispered Neil, and Emily giggled.

"I can't understand why anybody would want one!" she said, grinning. "Anyway, where have you been all morning?"

"I took Sam over the ridgeway. I've hardly walked him all week. I suppose I was feeling a little guilty," Neil replied, shoving both his hands in his jeans pockets. "I'm just popping in to see Muttley before the fireworks start!"

"It's going to be awful, Neil. What's going to happen?"

Neil looked blank. "Search me. I just hope everybody does what's best for Junior. Or Jason. Oh, I'm so confused about who owns that dog I keep calling him different names!" Neil shrugged and stomped off. "Oh, I'll see you later."

Muttley's pen had more locks and chains on it than Neil had ever seen before. He was surprised that the weight of metal and iron hadn't already been too much for the wire mesh and torn right through it.

Neil poked his fingers through the holes and said hello. Muttley's thick tail thumped on the wicker base of his basket and the dog whined gently.

"Poor Muttley. You've been through the ringer lately, haven't you?" Neil said sympathetically.

The dog responded with two quick barks and more thumps of his feathery gray tail.

"At least we got rid of the bows, old boy!" Neil waved good-bye, stood up and left the kennel block chuckling. Having Muttley at King Street had certainly been an experience. There was never a dull moment while he was around.

Neil stopped smiling as soon as he got outside. Turning into the Parkers' front driveway was Mr. Scott's Land Rover.

Neil froze and hoped the visitor couldn't see him yet. He wanted to see the look on Mr. Scott's face as he got out of the car, in order to judge what sort of mood he was in.

Neil studied the man's face closely but couldn't interpret his expression at all. He was relieved when Mr. Scott's wife also emerged from the car. He'd liked her; she had been so kind and friendly when they had visited Four Gate Farm.

Carole Parker greeted the Scotts on the driveway and took them through into the office. Neil followed and hoped his father's obedience class would finish soon. They were going to need all the help they could get.

"You've found Junior! That's excellent news." Neil entered the office just in time to hear Mr. Scott's delighted voice.

"The Westons should be arriving with him any

minute now," Carole Parker assured him, glancing at her watch.

"Are you sure they'll show up?" Mr. Scott asked suspiciously.

"Of course they will," said Neil, firmly. "They're not *bad* people, Mr. Scott. They love Jason . . . I mean Junior," he corrected himself quickly. "Probably as much as you do."

"That may well be true, Neil. But Junior is *my* dog. There's no escaping that fact."

Bob Parker popped his head around the office door and smiled. "Good morning, Paul. Thanks for coming. Mrs. Weston and the children have just arrived. Let's go through and meet them out back."

"Oh, good. Yes, let's settle this once and for all."

Neil followed the Scotts and his mother outside. He didn't like the sound of Mr. Scott's voice and immediately feared the worst. The Westons didn't stand a chance of keeping their former dog.

Pam Weston was standing in the middle of the stone courtyard. She had one arm around Jonathan, and was holding Kirsty's hand. Jason, the yellow Labrador, sat obediently in front of them panting.

"Junior! Here boy!" Mr. Scott knelt down on one knee and called his dog.

Junior pricked up his ears and looked in Mr. Scott's direction. There was only a brief moment of hesitation before the dog rushed over to greet him.

Kirsty Weston began to cry. She wiped her eyes with her sleeve and turned her head away.

"Be brave," her mother whispered, and handed her a tissue.

Mrs. Scott looked at her husband affectionately hugging the Labrador, and then at Kirsty. "Don't cry. You'll be able to see . . . Jason again, I'm sure." There was warmth in Mrs. Scott's eyes and Neil knew she meant what she said.

Bob Parker stood back with his arms folded. He seemed happy to let Mr. Scott and Mrs. Weston solve their problem by themselves. Neil looked on, too, but had a different feeling — one of helplessness. Suddenly he knew he had to speak up. He had to make sure Mr. Scott knew how it would affect the Westons if he took Jason away from them.

"Tell them why you gave him up, Mrs. Weston," Neil said quietly. "Tell Mr. Scott how much it means to Jonathan and Kirsty. Before he decides what to do."

Mr. Scott stood up and addressed Mrs. Weston. "I can see you're all upset. It must be difficult for you. Yes, tell me what did happen? Why did you get rid of him?"

Mrs. Weston told him the whole story. Bob and Carole listened, too, hearing the full details themselves for the first time.

Neil and Emily exchanged anxious glances. What would Mr. Scott do? Surely he wouldn't just walk away and take Jason with him?

Mr. Scott took a deep breath when he had finished listening to the story, then looked across at Neil's dad. "What do you think, Bob?"

Bob scratched his chin. "Usually, in cases where two people claim the same dog with legitimate reason the rule is to let the dog decide. Whoever he appears to know and like best is judged to be his owner. But in this case . . . there's really no question of a legal dispute." Bob Parker looked at Pam Weston. "The dog belongs to Paul. And he has every right to take him back."

"I know that what I did was wrong. And I'm sorry," Mrs. Weston said with emotion. "But you see, we all loved him so much."

A loud sob came from Kirsty. Jonathan was staring down at his feet, trying not to look at Jason standing obediently by Mr. Scott's side.

For a moment, Mr. Scott looked deep in thought and Neil suddenly knew he had the chance to influence his decision. "Mr. Scott? Can I say something?" he asked. Everyone looked at him.

"What are you up to, Neil?" whispered Emily, nudging him in the ribs with an elbow.

Neil ignored her and cleared his throat. "Let me get this straight, Mr. Scott. I know you bought him legally — I don't think anybody is doubting that. But can you tell me why you really want him?"

The directness of Neil's question surprised Mr. Scott. "Excuse me?" he said.

"Do you just want to use Junior for breeding and showing?"

"Well, yes. That's right," Mr. Scott confirmed, still looking a little confused.

"Did the judges at the Padsham Dog Show tell you why they didn't award Junior first prize in the Labrador class?"

"Yes, of course," Mr. Scott replied matter-of-factly. "They said it was because of that kink toward the end of his tail. It's not genetic. We think he was bitten by another puppy from his litter, and it caused a bit of damage."

Neil stared at Junior's wagging tail. He'd never noticed it before, but there *was* a kink in his tail that shouldn't have been there.

"It's enough to ensure he'll never qualify for a top prize in that case?"

Neil waited for a reply. If only he could make the Scotts agree to this point, then the next part of his plan might work.

"I suppose he'll never be up there with the best, no," said Paul Scott at last. "I think he won the second prize at Padsham on the strength of his personality. But it's precisely that happy, outgoing nature of his that I'd like to introduce into my future Labrador pups."

"So there *is* a solution here to keep everyone happy! One that nobody seems to have thought of. It might be best for Junior, too. After all, isn't that what everybody wants?" Neil said, looking around the sea of faces, all hanging on his every word.

"What is it, Neil?" asked his father. He looked mystified. "What are you suggesting?"

Neil took a deep breath. "Sharing him," he said.

Mr. Scott frowned. "What do you mean?" he inquired, frostily. "I'm not sure I like the sound of that at all."

"But Mr. Scott, it makes sense. You want Junior to help with your business. Mrs. Weston wants Jason as a pet. Well, there's no reason why he can't be both things to both people!"

Mrs. Weston was gazing at Neil with her mouth half open. Mr. Scott glanced at his wife and raised his eyebrows.

"I don't quite see how it would work, Neil," said Carole Parker.

"It's simple," Neil explained. He was sure the answer was more straightforward than everyone seemed to think. "Let the Westons look after Jason for the time being. You know they'll do a fine job, Mr. Scott. You've seen for yourself how much they love him, and how much he loves them. You said Junior isn't old enough yet for you to breed from him. When he *is* old enough, why can't you just borrow him back?"

Neil turned to Mrs. Weston, without waiting for a reply. "You would let the Scotts have him for a couple of days every so often, wouldn't you? If it meant you could keep Jason?"

"Of course!" Mrs. Weston confirmed with delight.

"How do you feel about it?" Neil asked Mr. Scott.

"Yes, how does Neil's plan grab you, Paul?" Mrs. Scott asked her husband, placing a hand on his arm.

Bob Parker looked at Neil and winked.

"I'm not sure. He needs to be kept in top breeding condition. He mustn't be overfed, or given the wrong diet for that matter," said Mr. Scott, sounding uncertain.

"You could devise a nutrition program for them to follow," suggested Emily.

"Yes. We don't mind doing that," Mrs. Weston said hopefully.

"Mr. Scott . . . ?" Neil gazed expectantly at the

man from Four Gate Farm and held his breath. Would he agree to the plan?

Mr. Scott was thinking hard. His brow was furrowed and he twirled his cap around in his hands. Then he cleared his throat.

"You were right about Jason, Neil."

Neil exploded inside. It was the first time Mr. Scott had called the yellow Labrador by his original name, Jason, and he knew that he was about to hear good news.

"Jason has a fantastic character and is a lovely dog. That's why I'm so attached to him. He loves human company and I must admit, we probably can't give him as much of that as young Jonathan and Kirsty might." He smiled at Kirsty and she brightened up, drying her eyes with the tissue.

Emily, too, sensed Mr. Scott was going to give in and gave the thumbs-up sign to her older brother.

"I think your plan is perfect, Neil," said Mr. Scott.

Everybody cheered and Jonathan and Kirsty rushed over to throw their arms around Jason.

Mr. Scott looked at Mrs. Weston. "I'd like you to consider having Jason on permanent loan. I'll give you plenty of warning when I think I'll need Jason at the farm. Until then, I think having such loving owners and a superb home will be the best possible thing anyone could do for him. And that includes me!"

Mr. Scott gave Jason a final pat on the head and smiled.

Bob Parker stepped forward and put an arm around Neil's shoulder. "Good work, Neil."

"Thanks. It *was* the best plan, wasn't it?"

"Definitely!" chorused Jonathan and Kirsty.

Jason swished his long pink tongue sideways and licked Mr. Scott on the wrist.

"He's saying 'thank you!'" cried Emily.

"Does this mean we really can keep him, Mom?" asked Kirsty, still bewildered by the unexpected and happy outcome of their visit to King Street Kennels.

"Yes, for ninety-nine-point-eight percent of the time, it does," confirmed Mrs. Weston, beaming.

"Oh, wow!" yelled Jonathan. "Jason's really ours again!"

Mrs. Weston blushed. "Thank you very much, Mr. Scott. I know I was a bit hasty letting Jason go in the first place and it was wrong of me to steal him. But thanks for giving us a second chance with him."

"Hey! Wait up, everyone! I forgot to tell you my good news!" Everyone turned and looked toward the barn. It was Neil's cousin, Steve Tansley, pulling his Labrador, Ricky.

"Steve!" gasped Neil. "What are you still doing here? Ricky's lesson finished ages ago!"

"I know. But I was trying to get him to stop chasing mice in the barn. You know how he's always doing stupid things!" Steve looked down at Ricky, who was sniffing at Jason, trying to make friends. Steve rolled his eyes. "Anyway, I forgot to tell you about yesterday!"

"Yesterday? Good news? What are you talking about, Steve?" said Neil, puzzled.

"Dad got Muttley to bark for him yesterday — before he brought him back here," said Steve, still grinning.

"Oh, no, Steve, not you, too?" Emily groaned. She knew exactly what was coming next!

"I know, I know. It was a crazy idea. But guess what? Five of the numbers came up in last night's draw! We're not millionaires, but we've won enough to keep my mom happy!"

"That's great!" said Neil, excitedly.

"It certainly is. Mom says it'll pay for all the things Muttley broke in our house last week!"

Neil laughed. "You're incredible, Steve!"

"I know. But not as incredible as dogs sometimes are. You should know that, Neil. I never understood why you were so interested in dogs. Now I'm beginning to understand."

Ricky barked loudly and Jason responded with a series of barks of his own. Suddenly the kennels behind them erupted in an uneven cacophony of barks and whines.

"Oh, no! You've set them all off!" Emily cried.

Everybody laughed.

"Dogs. Don't you just love them?" shouted Neil above the noise.

"Yes!" cried Kirsty and Jonathan Weston. "They're amazing!"